This story first appeared in *Jubilee Jackanory*, published by the BBC in 1977. It was then reprinted in a collection of stories by Penelope Lively entitled *Uninvited Ghosts*, published by William Heinemann Ltd in 1984.

This edition first published in Great Britain in 1993
by Simon & Schuster Young Books
Campus 400
Maylands Avenue
Hemel Hempstead
Herts HP2 7EZ

Typeset in 14/20pt Souvenir Light by Goodfellow & Egan Ltd, Cambridge
Printed and bound in Portugal by Ediçoes ASA

British Library Cataloguing in Publication Data available

ISBN 0 7500 1394 X
ISBN 0 7500 1395 8 (pb)

Penelope Lively

Princess by Mistake

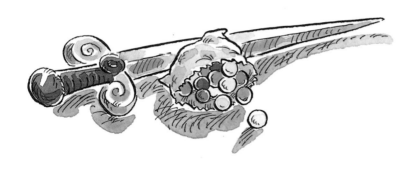

Illustrated by Julie Anderson

SIMON & SCHUSTER
YOUNG BOOKS

Chapter One

A long time ago, when I was young, on a Wednesday afternoon, a very strange thing happened to me. So strange, you probably won't believe it.

I know it was a Wednesday, because we always went to the library on Wednesday afternoons, my mother and my sister Sally and I.

And all the way home
from the library my sister Sally
and I had a fight. Sally said
I'd got a stupid lot of books –
they were all about aeroplanes
which was what I was interested in
at the time – and I said the ones she
had were boring and babyish. Fairy stories, they
were. Load of old rubbish! I jeered. Kings and
queens! Fairy godmothers! Princesses! And we
went on fighting each other all around the house
till suddenly my mother had had enough and she
turned us out.

So off we wandered, up the street, arguing away about one thing and another at the tops of our voices. We argued about who could run fastest and jump highest and swim best and then we got on to each other's personal appearance. Sally passed a few remarks about my freckles and I had a go at her long fair hair, of which she was excessively proud.

"Goldilocks!" I shouted. "S'pose you think you're the queen of the fairies! S'pose you think you're a princess!"

That was unwise, because Sally was very vain about her hair. She went bright scarlet and flew at me, and we rolled into the ditch together, scuffling.

It was the ditch outside Mr Crackington-Smith's garden. Mr Crackington-Smith was an elderly bachelor with a reputation for being difficult. He kept himself to himself and had awkward relations with his neighbours. Sally and I were so busy with our fight that neither of us saw him watching us over his gate, nor heard him say, "Will you kindly stop making that unpleasant noise outside my house."

Presently, though, we stopped for a breather and looked up and saw him scowling at us. He said, "Go away!"

And we sat there, all muddy and red in the face, and Sally said, very quietly, so quietly you wouldn't have thought he could possibly have heard, "Why should we?"

Mr Crackington-Smith said, "Because I'm telling you to. And if you don't," he went on, with a positive gleam in his eye, "I shall remove you."

We stared. Mr Crackington-Smith was quite a small man; we were rather large children. We heaved ourselves out of the ditch in silence, and shuffled about at the edge of the road. In fact we were just about to go, but Sally couldn't resist saying – to me, rudely, in a half-whisper – "I s'pose he thinks he's a magician or something?"

Mr Crackington-Smith took a pair of secateurs out of his pocket and started doing something to a rose. "As a matter of fact I am," he said calmly.

I sniggered.

Which was one of the stupidest things I ever did.

Chapter Two

After that everything happened at once. There was a great crack of thunder, and a flash of lightning. For exactly half a minute it rained very small toads; a number of black cats appeared on the garden wall and squalled horribly; broomsticks clattered around us like autumn leaves, and there was a loud thud of horse's hooves.

Sally gave a kind of squeak,
and I looked round to see her
being heaved, kicking and struggling,
on to the back of an enormous
black horse by a huge figure
in full armour wearing a crown.
"Help!" she bellowed.

I just had time to see, as the person arranged
her across the saddle in front of him, thrashing
about like a fish in a net, that she was done up in
full fairy-story princess gear – long frock, flowers in
her hair, the lot – and then the person dug his
spurs into the horse and away they went down the
road, sparks flying from the tarmac, Sally yelling
blue murder.

"Well," said Mr Crackington-Smith smugly, "satisfied?"

I said faintly: "What's he going to do with her?"

Mr Crackington-Smith was busy with his pruning now. "Oh, the usual stuff, I expect," he said. "Impenetrable dungeon with rats and snakes and all that. Standard fate of princesses. You'd better get on with it, hadn't you?"

"Get on with what?"

"Rescuing her, you stupid boy," said Mr Crackington-Smith irritably. He glanced at me and added, "I suppose we'd better give you a bit of the normal equipment."

There was a hiss and a clunk, and I found a very large heavy sword stuck firmly into my belt.

"Well," said Mr Crackington-Smith, "all the best." He put the secateurs in his pocket and began to walk towards his house.

I said desperately, "What do I *do*?"

Mr Crackington-Smith looked over his shoulder. "Oh, for goodness' sake!" he said. "Just the straight-forward routine! Impossible tasks; dragons and ogres and whatnot; spells; everybody *else* having an unfair advantage. Just do your best. The sword's a bit blunt, by the way. Oh, and I daresay you might find these come in handy too."

I felt something in my hands and looked down to find myself holding, in one, a packet of gobstoppers and in the other a folded-up comic. "How do I *start*?" I yelled.

His voice floated back through the closing front-door. "The Blue Star Garage, of course. He'll be turning that clapped-out old nag into a car by now. You'll know which by the usual signs."

The door slammed.

I set off down the road, the sword banging uncomfortably against my leg with every step. I passed one or two people I knew, but nobody gave me a second look: whatever was happening was happening only to Sally and me. The sword slapped my leg and glittered in the sunshine.

Chapter Three

I reached the garage. There were several cars being filled up with petrol, and a red van. The van-driver had his back to me, but the van had large black letters on it that said CASTLE DESPAIR PEST CONTROL SERVICE TEL. DRAGONSWICK 469. There was a sound of banging and shouting from inside the closed doors.

The driver turned to look at me, with an evil
grin; I saw the glint of chain mail under his
overalls. He got into the van, slammed the door,
and drove off at high speed.
I stood there, staring after it.

"Gracious me!" said a voice. "Don't just stand
there, boy. Get on and *do* something."

I looked round. There was no one about, but on top of one of the petrol pumps was a small green frog. Which, you must admit, is not at all the place you'd expect to find a small green frog. It all fitted.

I said to it, "How?"

"Put me in your pocket," said the frog. "I can see you're an amateur – you'll never cope with this on your own. Ouch! Don't squeeze! Now – we need transport. Hop on that motorbike."

"But I don't know how to ride it," I protested, "and anyway, I'm not old enough . . ."

"Oh, don't quibble," said the frog impatiently.

I got on to the bike – it was one of those great big fast Japanese ones – and it won't surprise you to hear, I imagine, that it went off just like that, obedient as a horse. I didn't have to ride it – it just went.

We roared down the road, and just round the first bend we caught sight of the tail of the red van disappearing over the top of the hill.

"There he goes!" said the frog. "Step it up a bit!"

I said, breathlessly, as the motorbike hurtled up to seventy miles an hour, "Who is he, anyway?"

"Gracious," said the frog, "how ignorant can you get? He's the Black King, isn't he? The fear and dread of all. Stops at nothing. Every crime in the book. Collects princesses. Got twenty-nine of them locked up at his place. Your sister's a princess, I take it?"

"No," I said, "she's Sally Smithers of 14 Winterton Road."

"Ah," said the frog with interest, "case of mistaken identity, then. Must be the hair that did it. He wouldn't stop to find out, anyway. Whoa there! They went thataway . . ."

Chapter Four

We screamed round another bend and suddenly, where there ought to have been the rather ordinary view of the outskirts of the next town, with rows of semis and a few shops and a school and that kind of thing, there was a great sweep of pine forest, with mountains behind and, bang in the middle, a huge castle straight off a pantomime back-cloth – all towers and turrets and slit windows and drawbridges and what-have-you. The red van was just whisking over a drawbridge and in at the gate.

We dashed after it, and as we arrived a few hundred yards from the castle walls there was a convulsive heaving of the ground and out of it sprang a thick undergrowth of thorn bushes, as impassable as anything you ever saw. "Here we go," said the frog, "up to his old tricks. Well, we can scupper that one, I reckon. Where's your sword?"

"Here," I said. I brandished it around uncertainly, and, would you believe it, even as I did so the blessed thing turned into a great big mowing machine, like my dad's only three times the size, with THORNMASTER SUPREME in black letters on the handle.

"Let her go!" yelled the frog, and I tore into the brambles with the mower and in no time at all we had cleared a path right up to the castle entrance. The motorbike had vanished.

The drawbridge was still down. I hurried across it, and just as we reached the open gateway there was the most appalling roar and out leapt the largest dog you ever saw in your life, with – yes, you've guessed it – eight heads, all splayed out from a great iron collar with a tag saying BOHEMIAN SECURITY SERVICES – YOUR PROPERTY IS OUR CONCERN. I took six paces backwards. "Get down, you brute!" said the frog. "Quick – tranquillise it!"

I said, "What?" and then I remembered the
packet of gobstoppers in my pocket. I pulled them
out and hurled one at each head, and the dog
snapped them up and stood there sucking and
gulping and quick as a flash we were past it and
into the great courtyard of the castle.

I stared round in perplexity.
There were a great many entrances,
and a nasty smell of mushrooms, and
black ravens all over the place, shuffling up and
down the parapets. The frog, from my pocket said,
"I predict an ogre. Keep on your toes. Be prepared
for evasive action."

Chapter Five

I slipped through the nearest doorway. Inside, there was a kind of entrance hall, very cold and damp, and amazingly, the doors of a lift with a panel of buttons beside it saying FIRST FLOOR AND BANQUETING HALL; WEST TOWER AND BOILING-OIL CHAMBER; BEDROOMS 1–489; THRONE ROOM and, finally, DUNGEONS AND GUEST ROOMS.

"So far so good," said the frog.

I stepped forward and pressed the button marked DUNGEONS, and just as I did so there was a kind of howling from down a long dark stone passage, rather like the noise of an approaching plane, getting louder and nearer all the time.

"Thought so . . ." said the frog. "Watch out!" and there in front of us was an immense ogre, with a great head of shaggy red hair, dressed in sacking, armed with a club studded with six-inch nails. The frog whispered, "Play it cool – they're not very bright, usually."

I said politely, "Good morning."

"Wurra-wurra-wurra-hhrumph . . . HOP IT!"
bellowed the ogre, advancing, and waving his club
around.

I side-stepped hastily and said, "I won't disturb
anyone. I was just going to pop down to the
dungeons and rescue my sister."

"Wassat?" said the ogre, scratching his head. He
didn't seem all that quick on the uptake.

The frog poked his nose out of my pocket and said, "No need to bother yourself with small fry like us – a fine strapping fellow like you."

"Grrr . . .!" said the ogre, flexing his muscles with ostentation. "Thirteen foot five in me socks; forty-one stone six pounds."

"Fantastic!" said the frog, nudging me. I edged towards the lift again, and pushed the button.

"Oy-oy . . ." growled the ogre. "Whaddya-think-yer-doing . . . HOP IT! SCRAM!"

"Amazing . . ." said the frog. "Thirteen foot five! Ever thought of tossing the caber? Javelin throwing? Olympic wrestling, that kind of thing?"

But it was the wrong approach. The ogre glared and began to rumble threateningly. "You think I'm some kinda dumb stoopid muscle man?" – I pressed the lift button as hard as I could – "You think I'm a bit thick or somefing? I'm a thinking man, I tell yer, I read books, I . . ."

"Absolutely," said the frog, "quite so. Obvious to anyone."

I groped in my pocket. "Here," I said. "Present for you . . ." and I flung the comic at the ogre as hard as I could.

He grabbed hold of it and a great beaming smile spread over his face. "Aaah!" he said. "Wow! Cor! Smashing!" He began to turn the pages over with his enormous fingers, and at that moment there was a whirr and a click and the lift doors slid open.

"Quick!" said the frog, and I shot into the lift and slammed my hand down on the START button. The doors slid shut again and the lift plunged down.

It stopped. The doors opened. I got out, cautiously.

Chapter Six

There was darkness, and stone walls streaming with water, and things that slithered off into the gloom, and flappings and squeakings and unpleasant smells. "Press on," said the frog, "this is the crunch. Himself will be somewhere about, I don't doubt."

I stumbled forward, calling, "Sally! Sally!" And after a minute or two, distantly, we heard a faint, answering voice. A number of faint, answering voices.

I rushed on, calling Sally's name, and the answering cries got closer and closer until at last I groped my way round a corner and there in front was a great padlocked door with an iron grille at the top, and Sally's face peering through it, shrieking, "Help! Get me out of here!"

"Move over," said the frog, "this is where I come in. Allowed one trick up your sleeve – it's all part of the game." And with that, he sprang out of my pocket, landed on the padlock, and turned himself into a small iron file which sliced through the metal quick as a flash. The padlock fell off, and the frog, looking a little sore around the mouth, reappeared poking his nose out of my pocket.

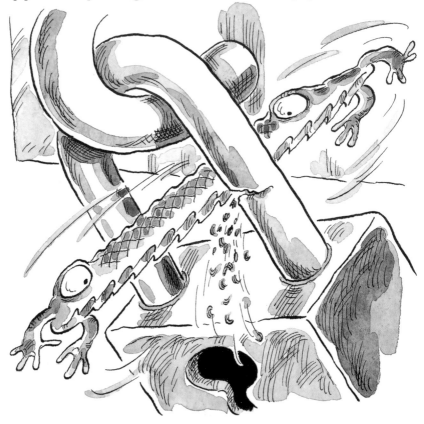

I flung the door open, and there was Sally, and a whole lot of other girls, all weeping and wailing and all in princess outfits. They fell on me in the most embarrassing way. And then all of a sudden there was a clatter of heavy footsteps in the passage outside. "Here we go!" said the frog. "It's up to you now! One thing – his backhand's weak."

It was the Black King. He sprang at me, armoured from top to toe, and I sprang back, with my sword in my hand (it said THORNMASTER SUPREME on the handle now – there'd been a slip-up somewhere).

We fought round and
round and up and down
and to and fro, with all the
princesses cheering like mad,
and twice I had him down and
once he had me down, and then, just
as I thought I couldn't go on a minute longer, he
gave a great howl and a banshee wail and there
was a puff of horrible black sulphurous smoke,
and he was gone.

We all streamed out of the castle, Sally and I
and the princesses and the frog in my pocket. The
princesses all said, "Thank you *ever* so much, that
was *really* kind . . ." and went dashing off in all
directions, and Sally and I leapt onto the
motorbike, which had reappeared again just
outside the castle, and we roared off too and . . .

Chapter Seven

There we were on the edge of the road outside
Mr Crackington-Smith's house. No motorbike, no
frog, no sword, Sally in jeans and a T-shirt again.
We looked at each other. Neither of us said
anything.

We walked home, very slowly, and we didn't say a thing but every now and then we glanced at each other, quick, and then looked away again. I knew. Sally knew. We still do. We don't talk about it, even now. It was a funny thing to happen, wasn't it – on a Wednesday afternoon. As I said, you'll have to take it or leave it, it's up to you – I'm just telling you what happened.

Look out for more exciting titles in the Storybooks series:

Judy and the Martian by Penelope Lively
Illustrated by Frank Rodgers

The Martian has only just passed his driving test, and is always losing his way. This time, he finds himself on planet Earth, hiding behind a freezer in a supermarket!

The King in the Forest by Michael Morpurgo
Illustrated by Tony Kerins

While a boy, Tod rescues a young fawn from the King's huntsmen. And many years later, Tod finds his loyalty to his old friend the deer put to the test . . .

The Midnight Moropus by Joan Aiken
Illustrated by Gavin Rowe

Jon knows of a strange story that, at midnight exactly, you can catch sight of a long-extinct horse at the waterfall. Jon becomes obsessed with the idea of catching a glimpse of the moropus . . .

Sam and Sue and Lavatory Lou by Robert Swindells
Illustrated by Val Biro

When Sam goes to the lavatory at the funfair and finds a ghost sitting on the washbasin, he gets the fright of his life!

Lizzie's War by Elisabeth Beresford
Illustrated by James Mayhew

When Lizzie's house is bombed during the war, she is sent to stay in the countryside with Miss Damps. How will Lizzie cope with her unfamiliar surroundings?

All these books can be purchased from your local bookseller. For more information about Storybooks, write to: *The Sales Department, Simon & Schuster Young Books, Campus 400, Maylands Avenue, Hemel Hempstead HP2 7EZ.*